DEATH BY CHRISTMAS FESTIVAL
SISTER SLEUTHS COZY MYSTERY

DONNA MUSE

Sweet Romance that Delights and Enchants!

Copyright © 2024 by Donna Muse

All rights reserved.

No part of this book may be reproduced in any form or by any electronic or mechanical means, including information storage and retrieval systems, without written permission from the author, except for the use of brief quotations in a book review.

PERSONAL WORD FROM THE AUTHOR

DEAREST READERS,

I'm so delighted that you have chosen one of my books to read. I have recently joined the team of writers at Tica House Publishing. Our goal is to inspire, entertain, and give you many hours of reading pleasure. Your kind words and loving readership are deeply appreciated.

Along with my fellow authors, I would like to personally invite you to sign up for updates and to become part of our **Exclusive Reader Club**—it's completely Free to Join!

Much love, Donna Muse

CLICK HERE to Join our Reader's Club and to Receive Tica House Updates!

https://cozymystery.subscribemenow.com/

CONTENTS

Personal Word From The Author	1
Chapter 1	4
Chapter 2	10
Chapter 3	15
Chapter 4	21
Chapter 5	26
Chapter 6	32
Chapter 7	38
Chapter 8	43
Chapter 9	49
Chapter 10	55
Chapter 11	61
Chapter 12	66
Chapter 13	72
Chapter 14	78
Chapter 15	83
Chapter 16	90
Chapter 17	94
Chapter 18	98
Chapter 19	102
Chapter 20	108
Chapter 21	115
Continue Reading…	120
Thanks For Reading	123
More Donna Muse Cozy Mysteries!	125
About the Author	127

[1]

CHRISTMAS COUNTDOWN - 24 DAYS UNTIL CHRISTMAS

"Maybelle how many more donuts are you planning on inhaling? That's like your third one."

Helen's exasperated tone reminded Maybelle that she never overindulged, and that was why she'd never been one to worry about her weight. But at the rate she was consuming donuts, chocolate, and ice-cream, she'd be rolling to the tree come Christmas.

Maybelle tossed the half-eaten donut back into the box and let out a sigh. "Thanks, eating my way out of humiliation probably won't work."

"Nope, besides, there's nothing to be humiliated about. He fooled you—he fooled all of us." Helen reached for her mug of coffee as she reassured her sister. "The important thing is that he's where he belongs."

"I just hope he stays there. His daddy is probably going to hire the best attorney there is, and he'll walk away with a slap on the wrist." Maybelle rolled her eyes at herself for falling for Drake Archibald.

If Peter and Helen hadn't found her, she would've been an icicle in the morgue by now. But they did find her, she reminded herself, and the killer was behind bars.

Usually after solving a case, she celebrated not only her skills but catching the criminal. But this time, she had allowed the humiliation to swallow her instead.

"Not likely," Helen pointed out. "He killed someone, Maybelle, and admitted it on tape. That's got to count for something."

"I just feel like a complete fraud. How can I pride myself on my intuition and my sleuthing skills after going away for a romantic weekend with a killer? Clearly my skills aren't what they used to be."

"Or this case was just different." Helen let out a wry chuckle. "You can't be right *all* the time."

Maybelle scoffed. "I don't like being wrong."

"Now you know what the rest of us mortal beings feel like," Helen teased. "Come on, it's over and done with, and it's time for us to move on to thinking about Christmas. You know the Christmas Festival is a little more than two weeks away, and we haven't even decided on a theme for our stall yet."

Maybelle's mind switched gears in an instant. There were few things she loved as much as Christmas. She couldn't think of a better way to forget about Drake Archibald and his deception than to focus on Christmas and a theme for their stall at the Christmas Festival.

"We've already had the candy cane theme, the winter wonderland theme, and last year we did Santa's workshop. We must come up with something unique, something that would lure in customers." Maybelle tossed some popped corn to her chickens. They were hanging out in their makeshift coop in the living room. Chicken Little did a swan dive to catch the first piece of popcorn, making Maybelle laugh.

"Actually, come to think of it, it's a good thing everything didn't work out with Drake. I can't imagine you having chickens in a condo, and I doubt he'd live in an old Victorian like this." Helen laughed.

Maybelle couldn't help but agree with a nod. "You're right. Anyway, back to the theme."

"Why don't we do something like Christmas in Hawaii, or wait, I've got the perfect theme: The Grinch." Helen's face lit up with excitement.

"Your idea for a theme for our Christmas stall is the grinch? Do you want us not to sell anything? Kids are terrified of the grinch." Maybelle shook her head as her eyes caught sight of a decoration that had been in their family for decades. There was a time when it had been used as an everyday utensil, but for the last half a century it was nothing more than a dust catcher, and a unique one at that.

"I've got it, Helen. Let's make our theme The Nutcracker." Maybelle got to her feet and retrieved the ornament from the display case. "These have become so popular in recent years, and they've become a symbol of Christmas. Did you know in the past they were symbols meant to keep away malevolent spirits and bring good luck?"

Helen frowned. "No, I didn't know that. I thought they were just part of the ballet."

Maybelle walked the doll over to Helen and moved the lever on its back. Its mouth opened wide, making Helen gasp. "See, you used to put nuts in its mouth and crack them open – thus the nutcracker."

"I'd be surprised if that still works. Still, I thought it was mostly just something they called tiny soldiers," Helen said.

"They are now, for the most part. But what do you think? We set up our stall around the theme of the nutcracker ballet, with sugar plum fairies and everything else. And then we stock the stall with vintage decorations. Christmas decorations from another era, like the glass baubles I sourced I last month."

Helen's eyes narrowed although Maybelle already knew her sister liked the idea. "So, you mean instead of just selling Christmas, we do it our way. Vintage Christmas?"

Maybelle nodded as a smile split her face in two. "A Vintage on the Vine Nutcracker Christmas."

"We should write this down." Helen was out of her seat in less than a second. She ran to the dining room and returned a few seconds later with a pen and paper. "What ornaments do you have in mind?"

"Firstly, we need to source dried holly, ivy, and bay leaves. Along with that we'll need dried orange slices. I know that's what they used to decorate empty branches in medieval times." Maybelle paced back and forth in front of the fireplace. "Red trucks. I know they've made a comeback, but we need to offer them in all sizes. You know the one with the tree on the back?"

"Yes, yes, that's a great idea, what else?" Helen asked, scribbling as fast as the ideas came to life.

"Glass baubles, tree toppers, wreaths with genuine bells instead of the plastic ones, and advent calendars. Not like the paper ones you buy at the store, but the wooden ones that become like a family heirloom..." Maybelle trailed off, running out of breath. "Are you writing all this down? If we want to do this, I'll need to start sourcing tomorrow."

"I've got it, keep going, you're on a roll." Helen smiled at Maybelle, relieved that her sister was finally thinking of something else other than almost being drowned.

"Snow globes, scented candles, gingerbread cookies, oh, and pocket watches. They were a common gift in Victorian times."

"We have quite a few in store as well. I'll start putting everything we have in store together for you then you know how much stock to order in. Just don't order too much, Maybelle, I know how you get when it's Christmas." Helen warned with a knowing look.

Maybelle laughed. "There's nothing like too much Christmas."

[2]

Detective Peter Nelson felt a little nervous walking up to the door of the old Victorian style house. He hadn't seen Maybelle since arresting Drake Archibald, and although he knew he saved Maybelle's life, he also knew her ego took a huge hit when she realized she had been dating the killer.

If she had been anyone else, he would've stopped by during business hours to give her an official update on the case, but after working with her on five cases, they had become friends.

Friends, Peter reminded himself. Just because they shared one amazing kiss when she saved his life, didn't mean she wanted to be more than friends. In fact, she'd made that clear.

Armed with a poinsettia, Peter knocked on the door.

"Snowflakes, we have to get those as well."

He could hear Maybelle's voice before she opened the door. She turned to him with a bright smile, seemingly happy and unaffected by what had just happened days ago. "Peter? Is that for me?"

Peter smiled. "Hello, Maybelle. Yes, I thought I'd bring a little something to get you in the spirit of Christmas and update you on the case while I'm here."

Maybelle accepted the poinsettia with a beaming smile. "It's beautiful. Come on in, we're sitting by the fireplace."

Peter followed Maybelle to the living room. "When you said '*we*' I thought you meant you and Helen. I didn't expect the chickens to be here as well," he said with a frown at the makeshift chicken playpen with artificial grass.

"Of course, they're here. Do you expect them to freeze their feathers off outside?" Maybelle asked as if it was a rhetorical question.

"They have their coop in the basement, near the furnace," Helen pointed out. "Hi Peter, coffee?"

"Thanks, Helen, though I'd rather not comment on the coop in the basement," Peter teased.

The Wright sisters had inherited the old Victorian house from their grandmother, but they had married modern and vintage perfectly to create a welcoming atmosphere from the moment a person stepped in the door.

Flames danced in the hearth, while the chickens pecked at popped corn on the artificial grass. Peter couldn't help but shake his head with a smile. He had never met anyone like Maybelle Wright in his entire life.

"So, what's the update on the case? Is everything wrapped up?" Maybelle asked, her smile fading slightly.

"He's being charged with murder in the first degree along with a few other charges that the DA are going to tag on. Regardless of what fancy attorneys his dad is flying in, it's safe to say he's going to sit for a very long time."

"That's a relief. It's good to know that Melanie is at least getting justice." Maybelle smiled with relief.

"Yeah, I think so, too," Peter agreed accepting the cup of coffee from Helen. "Thanks."

Peter spotted the pad of paper and realized he might have been intruding. The sisters might live together, but they also ran a business together. "Sorry, I didn't mean to interrupt. Were you having a meeting?"

Maybelle shook her head. "Not a meeting per se, but we were planning. We've decided on a theme for this year's Christmas Festival. We have a stall every year."

"Ah, the Christmas Festival. I've seen some flyers in town. Is that a thing?" Peter asked curiously.

Helen laughed. "The biggest thing since the Fourth of July if you live in Raven's Point. Every store in town has a stall. They turn the park into a Winter Wonderland, and everyone goes. In fact, the whole town is involved. The town council pays for the decorations and lights and everything else, but when it comes to setting up, everyone goes out to help."

Maybelle's eyes widened. "I completely forgot that's tomorrow. Did you remember to put a sign up on the door of the store?"

"Yes," Helen nodded with a smile. "I said we'd be closed for the day."

"Thanks, it completely slipped my mind." Maybelle turned to Peter. "You should come. We drag out the tables and the gazebos out of storage and everyone helps set everything up. Then on Monday, the decorating starts. You should see it, Peter. We really pull out all the stops. Fairy lights, tinsel, garlands, the whole nine yards."

"So, let me get this straight. You want me to come out on a freezing Saturday morning to help you setup tables?" Peter asked, not liking the idea at all.

Maybelle laughed. "No Peter, I want you to come out and join the community in getting ready for a holiday event. Who knows, you might even make some friends, if they can see past your sarcasm-instead-of-humor personality."

Peter chuckled. "Ha ha ha, at least I don't have to put dating-a-killer on my online dating profile."

Maybelle's eyes narrowed, pretending to be angry. "You're going to pay for that. First coffee for the morning is on you."

Helen laughed. "Oh joy, I don't even have to do anything, and already I'm getting free coffee. Please continue, hopefully you'll throw in a lunch as well."

Peter and Maybelle laughed, their gazes meeting. He enjoyed her company, and the attraction he felt for her was still there. But perhaps Maybelle was right. Perhaps being friends was for the best, because at least that way he had an excuse to stop by uninvited on a Friday night.

[3]

CHRISTMAS COUNTDOWN - 23 DAYS UNTIL CHRISTMAS

IN THE TOWN of Raven's Point, everyone didn't know everyone. Although for the most part, everyone knew *about* everyone.

As Maybelle stood in the town square waiting with her sister and the rest of the townsfolk who had come out to help setup for the Christmas Festival, she recognized numerous faces. Most of them she could tie a name to, and those she couldn't tie a name to were few and far between.

The paved town square in front of City Hall was adjacent to the town park. It was here where most events in town were held and where the town stored everything for those events. Maybelle glanced at her watch, realizing the mayor was running a little late. They should've started at nine o'clock, but it was already quarter past, and the mayor had yet to arrive.

It was tradition that the mayor made a little speech in which he welcomed everyone and explained what the town's goal was for that year's Christmas Festival. A small percentage of all sales were contributed to the town coffers every year for a certain purpose. The mayor usually announced that purpose on the morning everyone came out to help set up.

This year, Maybelle believed the mayor would apply the funds toward either new lamp posts on the main street or perhaps adding some benches to the park. Last year, the funds had been used to repaint Town Hall, and the year before that it had been used on a large advertising campaign to promote tourism in Raven's Point.

Some complained about having to pitch in, but Maybelle and Helen never did. They enjoyed getting involved and being part of community events to raise funds for the town. Not only was it a way to make a difference, but it was a way to keep your ear to the ground for any new developments that might arise.

"I think I'm getting frostbite in my toes," Helen complained as she rubbed her hands together.

"That's because those boots aren't leather. For this weather, cowhide is the only thing that insulates your feet from the cold," Maybelle pointed out. "You should've forced out the extra two hundred."

Helen scoffed. "But then I wouldn't have been able to afford the cashmere sweater."

Maybelle smiled indulgingly at her sister. Although their personalities were different in so many ways, they both loved treating themselves to shoes and cashmere.

Maybelle glanced around, wondering why the mayor was running late, when Peter walked toward her through the crowd with his hands above his head. He had two take-away cups stacked on top of each other in one hand and another in his other hand. A smile curved her mouth at his thoughtfulness.

She had teased him about the coffee last night, but apparently, he took it to heart.

When he saw her and a smile curved his mouth, Maybelle's heart skipped a beat. Drake had been a welcome distraction from the attraction she felt for Peter, but having saved her life, Maybelle was struggling to remember why she and Peter had agreed to be just friends in the first place.

"Three coffees as promised." Peter greeted her with a smile.

"I decided to try something a little different, so I hope you like it."

Maybelle accepted the coffee gratefully. "Thanks, I'm freezing."

She took a sip, and her brow rose with curiosity. "Is that cinnamon?"

"Cinnamon and maple to be exact. Part of the coffee shop's Christmas offerings," Peter explained as he handed Helen her cup.

"It's delicious." Maybelle approved with a smile. "We're still waiting on the mayor."

"Why can't we just get this done before we all lose our toes?" Peter asked, shivering slightly.

Maybelle laughed. "Yeah, we probably could, but he usually does a little speech."

"It's already been a half hour. I overheard someone say Fiona tried calling his wife, but she and the kids are out of town with her mother. So, she doesn't know where he is," Helen said. Fiona Charles was the town treasurer.

"But have they tried calling him?" Peter asked before taking a sip of his coffee.

"I can't imagine that they haven't." Maybelle shrugged.

Just then, Fiona Charles stepped up onto the small podium that the town janitor had erected for that purpose. "Hello? If I could have a word, please. Can everyone quiet down?"

A few murmurs passed through the crowd before Fiona cleared her throat and began to speak. "It seems Mayor Hoffman has been tied up this morning since we're unable to reach him. As soon as he arrives, we'll gather everyone. But for now, I think it's best if we get started. The mayor usually unlocks the storage unit after the welcome ceremony, but today we'll be asking Steven Jones, the town janitor to do the honors. Steven, if you would, please." Fiona gestured the town janitor to move forward through the crowd.

From where Maybelle and Helen stood, they had a clear view of the podium and the storage unit. It wasn't like their mayor to be running late, but Maybelle reasoned he had probably overslept or just forgot to charge his phone.

Steven Jones retrieved a set of keys from his pocket and walked toward the storage unit. He and Fiona exchanged a brief word before he slid the key into the lock and opened the doors.

The moment the doors opened, Fiona let out a shrill cry of horror. Steven suddenly stepped back, staggering slightly as his keys fell to the ground.

"Excuse me," Peter said immediately and pushed his way through the crowd toward the storage unit.

Maybelle shoved her coffee into her sister's hand before she was short on his heels. "Peter?"

"Something's not right," Peter called back over his shoulder.

They reached Fiona at the same time. "What's wrong?" Peter asked without wasting any time.

Fiona shook her head, her eyes wide with horror even as tears pooled in them. "It's the... mayor... He's...in there..."

The town janitor stood a few feet away, shaking his head. "His body is there..."

Maybelle followed Peter to the entrance of the storage unit and gasped when she recognized the mayor over Peter's shoulder. "He's dead."

"Yeah, no question about that." Peter nodded in agreement. "At least now we know why no one could reach him."

Maybelle felt a chill run down her spine. "There has to be foul play involved, because this door only locks from the outside."

Peter nodded. "I guess we've got another case to solve before Christmas, and this time a higher profile one than before."

[4]

Just last night Peter had left the Wright sisters and found himself looking forward to Christmas. For the first time in years, he wasn't in a busy station with a homicide department overflowing with cases. He could sit back and relax and simply enjoy the festivities of living in a small town.

But now, as he walked into the storage unit beneath Town Hall, he knew he had been wrong. For a moment, he had hoped that the mayor had died due to natural causes, but one look at the body proved differently.

And, like Maybelle had said, the storage unit could only be locked from the outside.

He took a few steps back, trying to retrace his own steps before he turned to Maybelle. "I need you to call the chief and let him know what's happened. We need to secure this crime scene before it gets trampled."

"What about the people?" Maybelle asked, glancing over her shoulder at the curious faces of almost every store owner in town.

"They're bound to find out sooner rather than later. Get up on that thing and tell them that we've discovered a crime scene. There won't be any setting up be done today."

Maybelle frowned. "Can't you talk to them?"

Peter stepped forward and touched Maybelle's hand. "I'm the only officer at a crime scene, Maybelle, I can't leave the scene, not even for a moment. I need you to help me with this."

Maybelle nodded. "Public speaking has never been my thing."

"It is today," Peter assured her. "You've got this."

Peter closed the doors of the storage unit, before positioning himself right in front of it. He watched as Maybelle took to the podium. It was the first time he saw Maybelle nervous, and he couldn't help but find her sweeter for it.

"Uh...hello? Can everyone hear me?" Maybelle asked over the microphone. "There's been a change in plans. We won't be setting up for the festival today."

People cried out their disappointment and fired questions at her from everywhere throughout the town square.

Maybelle nodded a couple of times before she held up her hand. "A crime scene has been discovered in the storage unit. Detective Nelson has it under control. For now, we're going to need to give the police space to do what they do best. Thanks for coming out, everyone."

Peter smiled at Maybelle when she joined his side again. "That was perfect. Thanks."

"I'll call the chief for you." Maybelle pulled out her cellphone. "What do I tell him? Won't he be surprised to hear from me?"

"He knows we work together frequently. Don't give names—just tell him there's an emergency we have to deal with right now." Peter rambled off as Fiona began tugging at his sleeve. "Yes, Mrs. Charles, is it?"

"Yes, that's right. Did my eyes betray me or was that ... the mayor?" She finished in a whisper.

Peter nodded. "For now, I'm going to need you to keep that to yourself. Someone will take your statement shortly, but until then, please don't answer any questions anyone might have."

Fiona Charles nodded and moved to one side. Her eyes were

cast down to the floor, clearly devasted by discovering the body of such a close colleague.

"The Chief said he's on his way," Maybelle informed Peter as she tucked her phone back in her coat.

"Good, can you keep an eye on the janitor for me? I don't want him talking to anyone."

"Sure." Maybelle nodded before she walked over to the town janitor.

Peter made a mental note to find out how many people had keys to the storage unit as he heard the sirens approach.

As soon as the first officers arrived, Peter stationed them outside the storage area before opening the doors again. He walked in, this time prepared for what he was going to see, trying to follow the same path he had before.

The body was lying a few yards from the entrance. Peter walked up to it and assessed the scene.

After a brief inspection, a few things were clear. Firstly, the mayor had been looking at the murderer when he was killed. Secondly, two shots had been fired. The first probably only injured him, and the second killed him.

Lastly, whoever killed the mayor had left him for dead on the floor surrounded by boxes of tinsel, fairy lights, and the banners that had hung over Main Street for the Fourth of July.

Peter slowly shook his head, realizing that in a town this small, the killer was mostly likely standing somewhere outside the door.

[5]

CHRISTMAS COUNTDOWN - 20 DAYS UNTIL CHRISTMAS

Maybelle had always thought that the speed at which news travelled in a smalltown was determined by the scandal factor. It was only now that she realized she had been wrong. Apparently, the mayor being murdered broke the speed of the light when it came to news traveling fast.

By Monday morning, the entire town knew that the mayor had been murdered. Instead of discussing the upcoming Christmas Festival, the entire town was speculating on who, what, and why.

Maybelle could hardly blame them, she realized as she pulled up to the police station on Tuesday morning. Everyone liked the mayor. Ever since his induction as mayor two years ago, Andrew Hoffman had done nothing but good for their town. He had increased the tourism in the area, focused on areas of improvement—based on the comments by the residents of Raven's Point, and he even managed to get Raven's Point highlighted as a tourism attraction on maps of the state.

So then why would anyone want to kill him, Maybelle wondered as she climbed out of her car. She wanted to stop by the station to talk to Peter the day before, but she knew with a case like this, he was probably up to his neck in red tape.

Instead, she had waited until this morning to stop by and find out if he needed her help.

As she walked into the station, the officer at the front desk recognized her and waved her through. She made her way to Peter's office and wasn't surprised to find him sitting behind his desk with three empty coffee cups and a look of confusion when she knocked on the door.

"I was wondering if you were going to stop by," Peter said, getting to his feet.

"I thought I'd give you a chance to go through the crime scene first, and deal with the red tape. I can imagine there is a lot of pressure coming from above on this one." Maybelle set down her purse and took a seat.

Peter nodded. "Yeah, it's even worse than I expected. He was a close friend of the governor, so you can only imagine the pressure I'm under. But look, it's almost Christmas and after what you've just been through, I can handle this one on my own."

Maybelle frowned. "You will do no such thing; he was my mayor, too. I'm getting to the bottom of this with you or on my own."

Peter chuckled. "Good to see you've got your fight back. I was worried there for a while."

"No need. So, what have you got so far?" Maybelle asked with a cocked brow.

"We couldn't find much at the scene, but as for the body, two bullet wounds to the head. Do you know of anyone who would like to hurt the mayor?" Peter asked. "I've spoken to his family and according to them, he was a saint. I went through his financials. The man is as clean as a bottle of bleach."

"Mayor Hoffman was a good man. A family man at that. His family has lived in town for generations, and except for the odd bit from the gossip mill here and there, I can't imagine anyone wanting to hurt him." Maybelle shrugged.

"Think, Maybelle, what bits about him reached you through the gossip mill?" Peter asked, slightly agitated.

He hated being under pressure to solve a case. He preferred letting things fall into place in their own time, but on this, there was no time. Christmas was barely three weeks away, and the mayor's family deserved answers before then.

"Firstly, there is Thomas Watson. He's not a violent man, but there were rumors about him being upset that Mayor Hoffman won the race to become mayor. This was the third time Thomas Watson stood to run, and I can't imagine he was happy to lose *again*."

"But that happened more than two years ago, right? Hoffman has been mayor for the last two years according to my information," Peter said.

"Yeah, but maybe Watson was waiting for the right opportunity." Maybelle shrugged. It was a watery guess at best, but it was better than nothing.

"Anything or anyone else?" Peter asked.

"Oh, there was that thing with Nicolas Evans last year. I don't know if it was true... wait, that was this year... Rumor had it that the mayor's wife was having an affair with Nicolas Evans. She didn't happen to mention that when you spoke to her, did she?"

"No, she didn't." Peter clenched his jaw as he made a note.

Maybelle could see Peter was grasping at straws. How did you find dirt or motive on someone that seemed clean as a whistle? "Peter, we'll find whoever did this. We just have to put in the work like we always do."

"I know," Peter nodded towards the empty cups of coffee. "And I have been, but still haven't come up with anything else."

"What about the town janitor? He had keys to the storage room. Doesn't that make him a suspect?" Maybelle asked, grasping at straws herself.

"Yeah, it does. Can you think of anyone else? What about Drake's friend, Bradley? Now with Drake looking at life in prison, Bradley's losing a lot of money."

Maybelle scoffed. "I can't imagine Bradley would have courage to do something like this himself. Besides, didn't he leave town after you arrested Drake?"

"Yeah, you're right. The accessory to murder thing didn't stick. Apparently, it's not a crime to date a girl under false pretensions." Peter scoffed. "So that leaves us with three suspects."

"For now," Maybelle assured him. "The more we dig, the more we'll find. We just have to work the case like any other. Keep going over every scrap of information until something clicks."

Peter smiled at her, making her heart skip a beat. "When did you become my voice of reason?"

Maybelle returned the smile, knowing that it was slightly flirtatious. "Good to know I have a voice—not sure if it's a voice of reason though."

Peter chuckled. "Come on, let's start looking at the backgrounds of these three, maybe something will pop up."

Maybelle nodded as she moved around the table to look at Peter's computer screen. She might have enjoyed Drake as a distraction, but as Peter's cologne filled her senses, she realized that even while she had been dating Drake, it had still been Peter on her mind.

[6]

CHRISTMAS COUNTDOWN – 19 DAYS UNTIL CHRISTMAS

After spending a couple of hours with Maybelle yesterday trying to find a motive for the mayor's killer, they had still come up empty.

This morning as Peter sat in his office, he wondered if he would ever have the opportunity to spend time with Maybelle outside his office or working a case. He shook his head, knowing that he needed to focus on the case, but Maybelle kept muddling his mind.

The attraction between them now felt even stronger than before after he had saved her life. If anything had happened to her...

Peter quivered at the thought of what he might have done if he had arrived too late. He might have been the one looking at a life sentence right now.

He made a few calls to get more information on the thin list of suspects he and Maybelle had come up with before he decided to head over to the morgue.

Ava Long, the town's medical examiner, was busy doing an autopsy on another patient as he walked in.

"Excuse the goo, I need to confirm a brain bleed." Ava set down the brain she was about to slice in half and smiled at Peter.

Peter usually had a strong stomach, but this time his stomach did a little bit of a nosedive. "Sure," he shrugged turning his gaze away from the brain. "I was hoping you'd have that report on the mayor for me?"

Ava's eyes widened with horror. "I *told* the IT guy my emails weren't working."

She stomped over to her computer and checked her outbox. "See there it is. And just yesterday he promised me all was well. I'm so sorry detective. Here, you can read the hard copy right now." Ava reached into a filing cabinet and drew out a file.

"No problem." Peter accepted the file and began to page through it. The start of the report specified the mayor's age, race, hair color, eye color and social security number. He leafed over to the report section of the document and let out a sigh. "No surprises here I'm afraid. Two bullet wounds, the second one was fatal."

"Yeah, the first pierced through a lung, but the second one ruptured the aortic valve." Ava shrugged. "I'm sorry, I know you were hoping for more information that could lead you to the killer."

"No fibers or anything else?" Peter grasped at straws again as he closed the file again.

"No, I didn't find anything out of place on the body, not even a trace of lipstick which I hoped would be the *coup d'état*. The only other thing that I could determine, was that his time of death was somewhere between five and eight on Friday evening. The body had been there for approximately twelve to fourteen hours when it was discovered."

Peter nodded. "Thanks Ava, good luck with your slicing and dicing."

Ava chuckled. "I'll tell you one thing. After finishing this patient, I'm not having cauliflower for at least a week."

Peter quivered at the thought as he left her office.

With nothing on her report, he still had little more than the three random suspects he and Maybelle had come up with initially. First things first, he decided, as he climbed into his car. He was going back to the scene of the crime.

A short while later, Peter lifted the crime scene tape, unlocked the door, and stepped into the storage area at Town Hall. It was a large area, at least half the size of Town Hall itself. Judging by the lackluster finish on the plastering, it was evident this area was never used for anything else but storage.

He walked past where the body of the mayor had been discovered into the depths of the storage dungeon, as Peter thought of it. There was a broken piano in the back, a few backdrops for stage plays, some that probably pre-dated him. There weren't any other entrances or exits except for the one door.

As he walked back to the where the mayor was found, Peter realized that whoever had killed the mayor either had a key or had used the mayor's key and tossed it afterward.

He kneeled and discovered two shell casings. They were a popular brand, so they wouldn't tie anyone to the crime scene. As for fingerprints, it was a long shot, but Peter bagged them anyway.

When he had first inspected the crime scene on Saturday, he

had looked for footsteps, but even now he couldn't find any footprints on the floor.

That was another thing that bothered him. He realized as he tucked the casings into his pocket after bagging them that none of the suspects he and Maybelle had come up with had a firearm. Although having a firearm and having a silenced firearm were two very different things, he mused as he looked around the storage area. Anyone could acquire a firearm if they knew the right people, or rather the wrong people.

As he walked out of the storage unit and closed the door behind him with a crime scene sticker. Whoever had killed the mayor had to have used a silencer. You couldn't shoot someone in the town square and not have anyone notice shots firing off—especially early on a Friday evening. People were coming home, walking down main street after stopping, some even going for a walk in the park.

He had put out a request for anyone who might have seen something to contact him, but thus far, he hadn't received any calls.

Which could only mean that nothing had looked out of place, or no one had paid attention because there wasn't anything to pay attention to.

Peter walked back to his car hoping that they had guessed

right with the suspects, because as for evidence, they had very very little to go on.

[7]

CHRISTMAS COUNTDOWN - 18 DAYS UNTIL CHRISTMAS

Unboxing an incoming shipment was one of the highlights for Maybelle as owner of a store. Setting her eyes on something unique for the first time made her heart skip a beat. But this morning as she took a scissor to the tape that sealed the box, there was no excitement at all.

Instead, her mind was rambling over the mayor's murder.

"What's that?" Helen asked, walking over as Maybelle sliced open the top of the box.

"Some nutcrackers I ordered last week before we even decided to use it as a theme for our stall," Maybelle explained.

"Ooh, will you let me see?" Helen asked eagerly as she peered at the box.

As Maybelle opened the box, she didn't experience her usual unboxing joy at all. The wooden soldiers looked back at her, as if mocking her for thinking about Christmas when there was a murderer on the loose. She picked one up, inspected the quality and approved it before she set it down again.

"I ordered four of each size. That way we sell them in sets of two," Maybelle explained, feeling as motivated as the lifeless dolls staring back at her.

Helen picked up a doll and walked over to the Bluetooth speaker. After doing something on her phone, *The Dance of the Sugarplum Fairy* began to play. Usually, Maybelle would laugh when her sister attempted anything in the form of ballet, but not even Helen's unsynchronized steps and stumbles could bring a smile to her face.

A minute into the song, the music stopped suddenly. Maybelle looked up to find Helen standing over her with a frown. "All right, this won't do. You're supposed to be jumping up and down for thinking ahead, and as for the quality, usually it would make you swoon. You're not even batting an eye. I need you excited about the Christmas Festival and these nutcrackers, Maybelle." Helen cocked her hands on her hips.

"If there even *is* a Christmas Festival. I can't imagine anyone would want to go anywhere near the town square after what happened." Maybelle sighed and closed the box on the nutcrackers, their faces disappearing into the dark. She knew that the festival was the last thing on her mind now, and she couldn't imagine it was different for anyone else.

Although your station in life didn't matter when you died, losing the mayor of a small town was a big deal. A big enough deal for everyone to call off Christmas traditions altogether. Vintage on the Vine always reserved a stall to be involved in the celebrations and the traditions, and Maybelle knew that there were stores that depended on the Christmas Festival to get them through the January slump.

"Maybelle, there *will* be a festival. It's a town tradition, it's what Mayor Hoffman would've wanted. At the risk of sounding like mom or grandma, go walk it off."

Maybelle chuckled wryly. "Walk it off. I have no idea where they even came up with that phrase. It's not like you can walk off your troubles."

"No, but you can take in a little bit of fresh air to gain perspective and to settle your mind. Now go on. Those guys don't deserve to lie in a dark box—they deserve to meet the rest of the Christmas decorations. I'll unpack them, and when you get back, I expect you to be in a better mood." Helen made it perfectly clear that although she might be the youngest sister, she was the one giving the orders.

Maybelle got to her feet. "Fine, I'll go for a walk, but I can't make any promises."

Helen didn't hesitate. She handed Maybelle her handbag. "Go on." She offered a smile as well.

Maybelle pulled on her red coat along with the blue and peacock green scarf she had chosen that morning before she slipped her handbag over her shoulder and walked out the front door. The cold breeze made her breath catch for a moment. She slipped on her gloves, grateful she had left them in the pocket of her jacket, while she decided in which direction she was headed.

She remembered what day of the week it was, and a mysterious smile curved her mouth as she headed west. Steven Jones, the town janitor, who had unlocked the storage room would be in the town park today, clearing out bins and picking up litter.

With purpose in her step, Maybelle quickly crossed from the one side of town to the other where the Town Hall and town park were. As she entered the snow-covered park, she was reassured that Steven was indeed there when she noticed the benches were all cleared of the light snow fall from the night before. She followed the path, her boots crunching the snow, as she went in search of Steven.

She was halfway down the path when she saw Steven clearing out a bin. For a moment, she simply stood and watched him. Was it possible that their town janitor, the sweet man who always waved and always had a word or two for anyone, was capable of murder?

Maybelle couldn't imagine that he was, but then how many murderers had walked away from suspicion because they were kind and not suspicious at all. For all she knew he could be a serial killer, disposing of body parts in the bins he cleaned down Main Street.

A shiver ran down her spine at the thought.

How did she just go from innocent to a possible serial killer?

Maybelle shook her head, trying to shake off the horrid thought.

She walked over to talk to him, but not before she reminded herself that this wasn't an official interview. If it was, Peter would be all over her for not notifying him of it first.

[8]

"Good morning, Steven." Maybelle walked up behind Steven with a smile.

"Miss Maybelle, good morning to you, too." Steven offered her a smile, with one front tooth missing.

How had Maybelle never noticed that before, she wondered as she searched his aged face. "How have you been after... after Saturday morning?"

Steven tied a knot in the bag he had just removed before he put it onto the back of the golf cart he used in the park. "A little disturbed, to be honest. Mr. Hoffman was nothing but kind to me, I can't imagine why anyone would want to hurt him."

Maybelle nodded. "I know. But I've learned that everyone has their secrets."

Steven chuckled and shook his head. "Miss Maybelle, I don't know about that. I'm an open book, no secrets with me. I've been in Raven's Point my whole life."

"You have? I never realized that. Didn't you leave for the army or anything?" Maybelle fished with expert subtlety.

Steven shook his head. "No, my mama used to say it's best if I don't do anything that strains my mind too much. She had the measles while she was pregnant with me, and that made me what mama use to say, a little slow. Nothing wrong with slow though," Steven quickly added with a smile. "I just take a little longer to learn new things."

Maybelle smiled easily, although she was quite shocked. "I'm sorry I never knew that."

How had she seen this man at least once a week for her entire life and never realized that he had a mental disability of some kind. Maybelle's heart swelled with empathy for the town janitor. She knew he had no family left, and now she couldn't help but blame herself for not showing an interest in him before.

She had sometimes wondered if he hadn't any ambition, because what else could be the reason for becoming a town janitor. But then, she realized that many folks might enjoy the job. Just because she wouldn't didn't mean a thing. Now, as she looked into Steven's innocent eyes, Maybelle realized that he shouldn't be on their list of suspects at all.

He hadn't explained exactly what kind of 'slow' he was, but it was evident from their conversation that he had the mind of a child in some ways.

"How could you have known Miss Maybelle? But it's a fact. I'm a bit slow. Your grandma used to know my mama; they were good friends. Miss Mabel was a kind woman, your grandma. She sometimes stopped by with a warm lunch on Sundays and this time of year, she often invited in me for warm cocoa. Can you make cocoa like she did?" Steven asked with a hopeful look.

Maybelle admired her grandmother even more for not ever telling anyone about how she looked out for Steven Jones. "I can't I'm afraid, but my sister can. But tell you what Steven, you're welcome to stop by the store anytime for something warm to drink, or something cold in summer. It might be instant cocoa, but I'll add extra marshmallows. How does that sound?"

Steven's face brightened. "Really, that'll be awfully kind, Miss Maybelle." He shook his head and pointed to the sky. "Mama always said becoming the town janitor would be a way for the whole town to look out for me, and she was right."

As Maybelle walked back to the store, she knew that Steven Jones wasn't possible of hurting a fly, much less killing the mayor.

The bells on the entrance of Vintage on the Vine jingled as she stepped inside.

"Are you in a better mood?" Helen asked meeting her at the door.

Maybelle smiled as she removed her coat and scarf. "Yes, I am. I ran into Steven Jones."

"The janitor?" Helen asked with a frown.

"Yeah, did you know he was…slow? I never realized. He said his mother had measles while she was pregnant with him and that resulted in him being a little slow."

Helen's eyes widened with surprise. "Hmm. I never knew. He's such a sweet man."

"Yeah, if you really start talking to him, he is a bit childlike. Did you know that grandma used to take him lunch some Sundays? She also invited him for cocoa whenever she had a chance." Maybelle shook her head. "I feel like I just discovered a side of grandma I didn't know about."

"She was a good person, Maybelle. And the first thing about good people is that they don't announce their good deeds for all to hear." Helen smiled.

Maybelle nodded. "Yeah, you're right. It's just... I was so wrong about him."

"You had him for a suspect, didn't you?" Helen asked with a wide-eyed look.

"Well, in my defense, he does have keys to the storage room." Maybelle lifted her hands defensively. "I invited him to come to the store whenever he felt like something warm to drink in winter or something cold in summer."

"That was nice of you. We can make him some instant hot chocolate and add some extra marshmallows like grandma used to do."

"That's what I said." Maybelle nodded.

"Good, now that that's settled. How do you like our nutcrackers?" Helen pointed to a shelf that caught your eye the moment you walked into the store.

Maybelle's face lifted with joy. "They look much better there than they did in the box. Don't you think we should get a set of bigger ones as well. At least three feet tall?"

Helen laughed. "And she's back! Sure, why don't you start sourcing them, and I'll put on some more Christmas music. How about some Hawaiian Christmas music?"

Maybelle laughed. "You know how much I dream to one day have a sunny Christmas. Why not?"

As Bing Crosby began to sing about how to say Merry Christmas in native Hawaiian, Maybelle dug into her browser bookmarks for suppliers of nutcrackers and other vintage Christmas ornaments.

[9]

CHRISTMAS COUNTDOWN - 17 DAYS UNTIL CHRISTMAS

Although he had three possible suspects, Peter still didn't have motive.

There were numerous ways to find motive in a murder case, but with this case Peter kept returning to the four 'Ls'.

Lust.

Love.

Loathing.

Loot.

Who benefited from the mayor's murder, who hated him, who coveted him, and who stood to lose everything?

That pointed Peter in the direction of one suspect.

Nicolas Evans.

Peter didn't know much about the rumored affair that Nicolas Evans had with Mrs. Mayor, but in his experience as a homicide detective, he did know that lust and love were often the likeliest motives for murder.

He hadn't mentioned the affair when he'd gone to see Mrs. Hoffman, but perhaps it was time he spoke to Nicolas Evans. Peter could go on his own, but he wanted to ask Maybelle to come. Not just for her sixth sense when it came to these things but for an opportunity to spend a little more time with her.

As Peter walked into Vintage on the Vine, he had to admit that his motives today weren't purely professional as he caught sight of Maybelle. She stood on her toes, helping Helen hang up a wreath. Just like always, she was a burst of color and variety. Her sweater was the color of butter, her pants the color of cherries, and they were paired with olive green leather boots. Her hair was tied up into a messy bun with a blue feather type thing, while red earrings dangled from her ears.

She turned, and their gazes met and for a moment. Peter could do nothing but smile. How was it that someone so colorful, so different from anyone whom he had ever dated could now catch his eye and make his heart skip a beat?

"Peter, we'll be with you in a minute," Helen explained as she fastened one side of the wreath before dashing over to Maybelle's side.

Maybelle walked up to him with a smile in place. "Good, now you spared me a trip down to the station. I was meaning to come and talk to you."

"You were?" Peter asked, surprised.

Maybelle nodded. "Yeah, come on back, and I'll tell you all about it."

Peter followed her into the kitchen and leaned against a counter. "So, what do you need to tell me?"

Maybelle's face lit up. "It wasn't Steven Jones."

"What? How do you know that?" Peter asked, already feeling a frown crease his brow.

"Because in every sense of the word except for his physicality and age, he's still a child. I spoke to him yesterday, and he admired the mayor. He wouldn't be able to hurt a fly. We can scratch him from our list."

Peter felt anger begin to simmer beneath the surface. "Maybelle, what did I tell you about talking to suspects on your own? You might be a consultant, but you can't put yourself in danger every time you feel like you know something."

Maybelle's eyes narrowed as she closed the distance between them and stopped right in front of him, her face only a few inches from his. If Peter wasn't the man his mother raised, he might have taken advantage of the opportunity to kiss her.

Maybelle could feel the magnetic attraction between them, but she ignored it as she reminded herself that she was about to scold him.

"I didn't go and seek him out and interview him purposely. Helen chased me out of the store for being in a bad mood. I went for a walk and happened to run into him at the park," Maybelle finished with a narrowed look.

Peter tilted his head. "Maybelle you can try and fool anyone else, but you don't fool me. You didn't just run into him. I appreciate you trying to help, but didn't you come close enough to being murdered on the last case?"

A shiver ran down Maybelle's spine as she remembered being in a beautiful mansion with a murderer. Her anger dissipated slightly as she realized Peter wasn't angry at her for talking to Steven. He was afraid she'd put herself in danger.

A slow smile curved her mouth. "You're concerned for my safety, aren't you?"

Peter's eyes widened slowly before he downplayed his feelings again. "Of course, I am. As an officer of the law, I'm concerned for everyone's safety."

Maybelle knew she was playing with fire, but she stepped even closer to the flames. "I promise I won't do anything to upset you again, Officer," she said with a pretend southern accent.

Peter's eyes darkened. "Don't do that."

He stepped away a bit. "I'll talk to Steven myself to confirm, but in the meantime, I'm heading over to surprise Nicolas Evans with a visit. I was hoping you could join me."

Maybelle's mouth curved into a smile. Just because they had agreed it was best to be friends, didn't mean she couldn't enjoy a little harmless flirtation. "Of course, I'll go with you. When did you have in mind?"

Peter looked at her, his eyes back to their normal hue of blue. "Now, if you're not too busy."

Maybelle turned with a flourish. "For you, I'm never too busy."

She walked out of the kitchen sashaying just a little, knowing that Peter was following her. If she was going to spend the weeks leading up to Christmas solving a murder, who said she couldn't have a little fun whilst doing it?

Seeing Peter all worked up had been even more exciting than putting in an order for two three-foot-tall nutcrackers.

[10]

As Peter switched on the engine with Maybelle seated beside him in his truck, he reached for the AC controls and turned down the temperature.

Maybelle turned to him with a look of horror. "It's freezing outside. Is there a reason why you want it to be freezing in here as well?"

Peter shrugged. "I'm a little hot."

Maybelle's laughter was more flirtatious than she intended. "Do I make you all hot and bothered, Detective Nelson?"

Peter knew she was just teasing him, but it didn't help the fact that he wanted to do nothing more than crush his mouth against hers.

Instead, he put the truck in reverse and backed out onto Main Street.

Although both he and Maybelle were quiet on their way to where Nicolas Evans worked as a manager of a furniture store, the air in the truck cracked and sizzled between them.

For a man who had dated frequently in his younger days, and even had a serious relationship or two, the connection he felt with Maybelle was completely something new. He had never felt the need to simply look at someone to try and see what they were thinking.

He had never met anyone that could take him from zero to anger in less than a second and from anger to laughter even quicker. She was like a phenomenon to him, not just another woman. He pulled up in front of the furniture store and climbed out.

Maybelle met him in front of the truck. "So, how do you want to go about this?"

"You just keep quiet and follow my lead." Peter led her to the door and opened it for her to walk in ahead of him. "We're doing this my way," he mumbled behind her.

The security guard welcomed them at the door.

"I'm looking for Mr. Nicolas Evans. I'm with the Raven's Point PD," Peter flashed his badge, and it earned him the desired response. The security guard's eyes widened with surprise before he nodded.

"This way, sir."

Peter and Maybelle followed him to an office in the back. The blinds were closed so they couldn't see inside, Peter would've preferred if they had been open.

A few moments later, the guard showed them into the office.

"Detective Nelson, isn't it? Please, come in," Nicolas Evans said with suave smile.

Everything about him was suave, from his fashionable haircut, his silk tie, right down to the fancy watch on his arm. A man like this didn't date a woman simply because he could; he liked a challenge.

Peter knew that dating the mayor's wife had been more about the challenge than the woman herself.

"Thank you. This is Maybelle Wright. She's consulting on the case." Peter took a seat without hesitation. Maybelle did the same.

"Case?" Nicolas asked, taking a seat, before smoothing down his tie.

"The murder of Andrew Hoffman. I'm sure you've heard," Peter explained in his most professional tone of voice.

"Ah, yes. I heard. Tragedy, isn't i?. He was such a good man." Nicolas was clearly trying his best to sound sincere.

"He couldn't have been that good of a man if his wife was messing around with you." Peter dropped the bomb without preamble.

Nicolas shifted in his seat uncomfortably. "Look, I don't know what you've heard, but that's been over for ages."

"Really? How long do you see as… ages?" Maybelle cocked a brow as she crossed her arms.

"Four, no, I think three months at least." Nicolas shrugged. "It wasn't that serious between us, honestly."

"That's not what I heard," Maybelle jumped in. "From what I heard you two were planning on running off together."

Peter didn't know if Maybelle was telling the truth or improvising, but he liked it.

Nicolas let out a heavy sigh, and the suave façade he had in place suddenly fell away. "Is that why you're here? You think I had something to do with Andrew's murder because of my relationship with Cecilia?"

Peter shrugged. "Ah look, you connected the dots."

"Why don't we try this again. Tell us about your relationship with Cecilia." Maybelle shifted forward in her seat.

"It just happened." Nicolas shrugged. "She came in a few times. We got friendly, and one thing led to another. Neither of us expected it or planned for it."

Peter glanced at Maybelle and realized that was exactly what was happening between them. He shoved the thought aside and turned his attention back to the suspect.

"I asked her to divorce him. I told her we could move and start a new life together, but then... Andrew walked in on us. I thought that was the end of their marriage, but the fool insisted on marriage counseling. Cecilia agreed to give him three months...." Nicolas dragged a hand over his eyes. "She called me last month to tell me she loved him, and she didn't want a new life; she wanted to continue the life they had built together."

"That must've been rough." Peter nodded.

"Yeah, it was, but I respected her decision. If you think I went all haywire on emotions and jealousy and killed the man, you're wrong," Nicolas pointed out defensively.

"Then that makes things easier for us. As soon as you can provide us with an alibi for Friday night between five and ten, we can cross you off our list." Maybelle got to her feet. "And just so you know, being alone doesn't count as an alibi."

Peter stood up, glad that Maybelle had pointed it out with such frost in her voice. "Thanks for your time." He dropped a card on Nicolas's table and gestured to Maybelle to walk through the door first.

They walked out of Nicolas's office without even looking back. But the moment they climbed into the truck, Peter turned to Maybelle with a look of astonishment. "We make one heck of a team."

Maybelle laughed. "I know. Wasn't that fun?"

Peter shook his head. "Only you would think questioning a suspect is fun." He gunned the engine and turned to her again. "What do you think? Do you think he's good for it?"

"I don't think he has courage for anything else than chasing skirts to be honest, but let's wait and see what he comes up with as an alibi."

Peter nodded in agreement. "Yeah, let's do that."

[11]

CHRISTMAS COUNTDOWN – 15 DAYS UNTIL CHRISTMAS

"We are going to have the best stall at the festival this year. It's a shame they don't hand out awards for the most innovative or best decorated stall," Helen said with a sigh as she unboxed another shipment of nutcrackers, this time with ballerinas as well.

Maybelle nodded as she began crating up the decorations they were going to sell at the Christmas festival. "What if we don't have the festival?"

"We will. I spoke to Fiona Charles, the treasurer. She said they have already spent the money on the decorations and hiring Santas. It would go to waste if the festival were cancelled now." Helen picked up a tiny ballerina tree decoration and sighed. "Isn't this just darling?"

"And you know this for certain, that it's not going to be cancelled?" Maybelle asked, hating that her sister was more in the know. Usually, it was Maybelle who was up to speed with everything when it came to Vintage on the Vine, but she was so distracted with solving the mayor's murder, that she hadn't even thought to query about the festival.

"Yes, Maybelle," Helen said impatiently. "I even checked with some of the other store owners. Apparently, the decorators are starting two days before the festival. It's going to be tight, but they are waiting for the crime scene to be cleared by Peter."

"Yeah, I'm not sure if he's going to do that until we've solved the case." Maybelle set down the decorations and turned to Helen. "We still don't know who could've had motive. Our list of suspects is more hopeful, than motive-driven, and as for the weapon, it's such a general firearm, it could've been anyone."

"Then don't look at anyone in particular—look at everyone. Everyone the mayor did business with, people from his past, people from his present, and most of all, people who were in contact with him before his death. Didn't he have an appointment book you could go through?"

Maybelle's eyes lit up. "Helen, you're right. We've narrowed our suspect list because we're in a rush, but that doesn't mean there aren't other suspects. The appointment book is a good place to start. I'll make sure Peter finds out who has it. If it's at his office, Peter probably already has it, but if it's at home, he'll need to speak to Cecilia Hoffman."

"Great, now that you've got a plan, can we get back to what we're selling at the Christmas market? I'm afraid we don't have enough items to stock our stall." Helen glanced around the three crates they had packed thus far.

Maybelle nodded. "We could add some vinyl records. We got a few on that estate sale a while back. I think there was Bing Cosby and Boney M in it. We have grandma's copies, so we can sell those."

"Vinyl's are a great idea. What about bits and bobs. Like Christmassy pens and stationery, gift labels, maybe even some Christmas hats, ooh, what about stockings?" Helen asked excitedly.

Maybelle laughed. "You're really into the spirit of Christmas this year, aren't you? Sure, go ahead and get some bits and bobs. But you'll have to get them locally, otherwise I'm afraid we don't get them in time."

"You've got it." Helen nodded. "Now, why don't you go and

see Peter? The sooner you solve this case, the sooner I get my business partner back."

Maybelle couldn't help but agree. "You're right. Thanks for understanding."

A short while later, Maybelle walked into Peter's office. "There's one thing we haven't looked at, the appointment book."

Peter looked up from his desk. "The appointment book?"

"If anyone had a problem with the mayor, surely, they would've gone to see him. Perhaps he had an appointment with the killer a week before his death? Do you know if it was with the things you took from his office?"

Peter frowned. "No, there wasn't an appointment book, but I can give his wife a call. We might get lucky, and the mayor might have been one of those guys who keeps record of everything that happens every day in his life."

"Exactly, a note or a name, anything could give us more than we have at the moment." Maybelle agreed.

"But first, we can interview Thomas Watson. I think we should go and see him tomorrow. Will Helen be able to spare you at the store?"

"Yeah, I'm sure she'll be fine. She's preparing for the Christmas Festival as if there hadn't been a murder at all.

Whereas I find it hard to believe that they're going to go ahead with it at all. Apparently, you haven't even cleared the crime scene yet?"

Peter nodded. "Yeah, I had some city folks come in to run the scene again. They're in there today—they'll be finishing up tomorrow. After that, I should have no reason not to clear the scene."

"Good because you do realize a Christmas Festival without Christmas decorations is just another market day?" Maybelle cocked her one brow.

Peter chuckled. "Just like you to blame me for ruining the Christmas Festival because I need to solve a murder. There is just no winning with you is there?"

Maybelle felt a light blush color her cheeks as her heart skipped a beat. "There is sometimes, but that doesn't mean a win comes easily."

Peter flashed her a dashing grin. "Maybelle Wright, if I've learned anything it's that nothing with you comes easily."

[12]

CHRISTMAS COUNTDOWN – 14 DAYS UNTIL CHRISTMAS

Men like Thomas Watson, who held a political profile, didn't like being interviewed by the police. Peter also knew that he'd rather be forthcoming and make it a onetime visit, if the interview was done at the police station in an interrogation room.

On the other side of the mirror glass, Peter turned to Maybelle. "We'll let him sweat for a few minutes."

Maybelle laughed. "This is cruel. You could've just interviewed him in your office."

Peter shrugged. "He'll talk easier if we do this the official way. You'll see."

Maybelle doubted him, but Peter didn't care. Maybelle doubted him a lot these days, just like he doubted her, but somehow their mutual doubts always resulted in solving a case.

Peter knew that the whole town was eager for the decorating committee to start preparing for the festival, but he also knew that having the crime scene unit in there was the best thing he could do. They had equipment and gadgets that picked up things the naked eye could never see, and hopefully in this case, they picked up something that gave them more information on Andrew Hoffman's killer.

"All right, he's waited long enough," Peter said to Maybelle before he led her out the door and into the interrogation room.

"Mr. Watson, I apologize for having you meet with me here. I simply couldn't carve out the time to come and see you, and as for the location," Peter glanced around the pale grey walls, "the Chief is having a Curb the Crime thing with the patrol officers in the board room. This was the only other option."

Thomas Watson straightened his tie. "I don't mind. I'm happy to help in any way that I can."

It was the general understanding of the entire town that now that Mayor Andrew Hoffman was gone, Thomas Watson would run unopposed in the next election. He wore his suit as if he had already won the mayoral election. It just didn't sit right with Peter.

"Sorry, let me introduce you to Maybelle Wright. She's consulting with the department on this case." Peter gestured to Maybelle.

Thomas frowned. "A police department that consults with shop owners, surely the town could afford another detective if that is where the problem lies?"

Peter sat down across from Watson, feeling Maybelle tense beside him. "We don't need another detective. Besides, Miss Wright has proved to be a canyon of information with an instinct like a bloodhound. We only call her in to assist on the bigger cases."

"And Andrew's case is big because of what? Because he was the mayor?" Watson snapped agitatedly.

Peter nodded with ease. "Yes. As the mayor, town guardian, and spokesperson for Raven's Point, I'm sure you can understand that his case is considered 'big'. In such cases, especially with political figures, we always need to ensure there wasn't an underlying political motive, or an act of domestic terrorism involved."

Watson's eyes widened marginally. "Domestic terrorism?"

"That's right," Maybelle said with a smile. "That's when someone tries to disrupt the chain of command or safety within the borders of the United States."

"Look, I don't know what you think you know, but I had nothing to do with Hoffman's murder."

"That is yet to be determined." Peter sat back and crossed his arms. "You were his nemesis, his only opponent in the race for mayor. And now with him gone, you probably can't wait to step into his shoes. A little convenient, considering the polls were already leaning in his favor to be reelected next year."

Watson shook his head. "I didn't do this. I promise you. When was he killed … Friday night? Right? I was at a card game with some businessman. Here, take my phone. Call Walter Suzek, Lee Yong, and Adolfo Rinaldi. We play once a month. The game starts around four and goes on until late. I only got home after eleven on Friday night."

Peter passed the phone to Maybelle. "Would you mind making those calls?"

Maybelle nodded and excused herself from the room.

Peter knew that Watson was telling the truth, but that didn't make him like the man. Thomas Watson was an opportunistic politician, and he'd met quite a few of those in the city. His type was someone who couldn't get the polls to favor him, so he waited for someone to fail before he jumped onto their demise.

Maybelle returned a few minutes later, giving Peter a nod before handing the phone back to Watson.

"Your alibi checks out Mr. Watson, but that doesn't mean you're in the clear. Make any large payments recently? For say... a hitman?"

Watson got to his feet; finally the man showed an inch of courage. "This is preposterous. You have my alibi, and I won't answer that ridiculous question. If you have any evidence that links me to this murder, feel free to contact my attorney."

He walked out of the interrogation room, leaving with his cloud of anger.

"It wasn't him," Maybelle said turning to Peter.

Peter nodded. "I know. I was toying with him because we've got nothing else to go on."

Peter's phone rang, and he apologized to Maybelle before he answered it. After a few brief words he hung up and turned to Maybelle with a baffled look.

"That was the crime scene unit chief; they found something at the scene," Peter began. "Although they were faded and hard to size, they found evidence of high heels stepping around Hoffman's body."

"High heels?" Maybelle asked surprised. "That doesn't make any sense at all."

"No, it doesn't. That either means we don't have the right suspects, or our killer had a female with him at the time of the killing."

"Or the woman did the killing."

Peter and Maybelle were both lost as to the new evidence. None of their suspects were female, and except for Hoffman's wife, they hadn't even interviewed a female in the entire case.

[13]

CHRISTMAS COUNTDOWN - 12 DAYS UNTIL CHRISTMAS

"Maybelle, the love of your life has arrived," Helen called out at the top of her lungs when the doorbell began to chime jingle bells.

"How did you hack into the doorbell?" Maybelle laughed on her way to the front door. "And please, no one must know about the love of my life. It's a secret, until I say differently."

Maybelle opened the door and wished that the floor would swallow her whole when she met Peter's look of intrigue.

"The love of your life…?" Peter asked, slapping that charming smile on his face that made Maybelle's knees wobble just a little.

"That wasn't, it isn't… Pizza!" Maybelle cried out wishing that her cheeks weren't aflame with humiliation. The last thing she needed was for Peter Nelson to believe he was the love of her life. Although he had the power to render her speechless, make her knees wobbly and make her blush when he flirted with her, that didn't mean anything.

"What?" Peter asked confused.

Maybelle nodded, covering her face with her hands. "Pizza. We were talking about pizza. The love of my life is pizza. We ordered some, and we thought… when the doorbell rang…"

Peter burst out laughing. "You thought I was the pizza guy."

"Yes." Maybelle flinched as she met his gaze. "Just come in, and don't make this anymore awkward than it already is."

"Oh, hi, Peter." Helen laughed as Peter walked into the living room. "Heard all that, did you?"

Peter chuckled. "Most of it. I must say… I was intrigued."

"Oh, stop it, both of you," Maybelle said impatiently when the doorbell began to chime again. "Helen, your turn."

"I can wait. I mean I don't want to interrupt a date between you and the love of your life," Peter teased.

Maybelle groaned. "One more word out of you, and you don't get a slice."

Peter pretended to zip his lips.

Helen returned with two boxes of pizza and set them down on the coffee table. "We have spicy 'C', with extra cheese, and this one is pepperoni with extra cheese."

"Right." Peter nodded. "Spicy 'C'." He glanced at the chickens pecking at feed in their winter playpen.

"Don't you dare." Maybelle pointed a finger at him. "You know the rules."

Peter laughed. He knew that the word chicken was off limits when it came to food around Maybelle's chickens. "I wouldn't."

Once everyone had a slice in hand, Maybelle took her spot on the reclining chair that looked as if it came from the seventies. She rested her socked feet on a footstool and took a bite of pizza. A quiet moan escaped her as she closed her eyes and savored the taste.

Peter turned to Helen. "Now I get it, the love of her life."

Helen nodded. "So far, the only uncontested winner of Maybelle's heart."

Maybelle was so focused on her slice of pizza she didn't even hear them, or she was just ignoring them. Peter decided it would be best to wait until Maybelle was done with her pizza before he brought up the reason for his visit.

After another slice of pizza, wine was poured, and Maybelle returned to her seat with a glass of wine in hand. "I'd like to think you didn't just come over to snag some pizza?"

Peter shook his head. "Nope. I came to tell you that the alibi for Steven Jones checked out. We both knew he didn't do it, but now he's officially off the list. That leaves us with the enemy and the adulterer."

"Who claim to have alibis," Maybelle pointed out.

"And with the information from the CSU, we have female footprints as well." Peter nodded in agreement.

"Did the appointment book bring up anything?" Maybelle asked with a frown before taking as sip of her wine.

Peter shook his head. "Nothing that stood out. To be safe, I've requested background checks on everyone he had meetings with in the last ten days before the murder. I'm sure it's a waste of time, but hopefully something shows up."

"Sounds to me like the two of you have come across the perfect murder." Helen looked at Maybelle before she turned to Peter. "No fingerprints, no evidence, no motive, and a crime scene that's just about clean."

Maybelle and Peter answered her as if they were one person. "There is no such thing as the perfect murder."

"Good, just checking to make sure you're still on top of your game." Helen smiled over her glass of wine.

"We're missing something. I'm just not sure what it is." Maybelle shook her head.

"Apparently, Albert Eggstein is in the mood for spicy 'C'." Peter began to laugh as Albert Eggstein flew the playpen and walked over to the box of pizza.

"Albert, no!" Maybelle was on her feet in a second. "I think it's time for you to go to bed."

Before Peter knew what was happening, Maybelle had opened the gate of the indoor playpen, and she was herding her chickens downstairs to the basement.

He turned to Helen with a baffled look. "And they just let her herd them like that?"

"Yup, every night. I'm telling you. She would've made a great border collie."

Peter began to laugh, and Helen joined in. When their laughter died down, Peter shook his head. "There simply is no one like your sister, is there?"

Helen agreed. "Not that I've met, and I've met quite my share of people in the store. You have all types when it comes to vintage collectors."

"I can only imagine," Peter said before taking a sip of his wine.

He had come to talk about the case, but instead, he was enjoying a glass of wine by the fire and learning more about the woman who occupied his mind whenever he wasn't thinking about his work.

[14]

CHRISTMAS COUNTDOWN – 11 DAYS UNTIL CHRISTMAS

"Thanks for meeting me here," Maybelle said as Peter joined her at Town Hall.

"I don't know what you think you're going to find that the CSU couldn't find. You read the report last night. They didn't get anything but the footprint." Peter unlocked the storage unit that would be cleared after their visit for the decorators to come and start decorating for the festival.

"I know, and I don't think I'm going to find anything either. I'm just hoping by being in there, I'll get a better feel for what happened. I always go with my gut, and last night I dreamt about coming in here. It might be nothing, but Peter, what if it's something? It's not like we have anything else to do but sit around and wait for a suspect to turn themselves in." Maybelle stepped into the storage room, and her breath caught.

She had been at crime scenes before, but for some reason, this time it gave her an eerie feeling. She walked in ahead of Peter and glanced around the dark and musty dungeon. "I wonder what this was used for before… like a hundred years ago?"

"In my experience, probably cells for prisoners." Peter shrugged, following her in. "That's how they used to do it."

"Probably … that's probably why it feels so eerie down here." Maybelle stopped at the spot where the mayor had been found and turned around to look at the entrance of the storage room. "The killer had to have been what, six or seven feet from the mayor?"

"Yeah, best guestimate was six, although the first shot could've been closer." Peter nodded.

"These boxes are dented," Maybelle said, running her hand over a cardboard box marked Easter.

"Most of the boxes in here are dented. Why, what are you thinking?" Peter asked.

Maybelle shook her head and walked to the entrance. "I'm not sure."

She stood at the entrance, and she was taken back to her dream the night before. She began to draw on all the information they had and saw the murder playout before her eyes.

"I think I know what happened," Maybelle said, gesturing Peter to come to her.

"How?" Peter asked confused.

Maybelle shrugged. "Look, the body was there, and the boxes beside it are dented. I think he was shot at close range, but he wasn't killed just yet. I think the mayor fought back. Whoever his assailant was fell onto those boxes. They must have regained their footing and ran for the door, stopping just long enough to shoot the mayor again."

Peter frowned. "If the dented box plays into the murder, then you might be right. That would explain why the shots weren't fired from the same distance."

"Exactly. Andrew wasn't a tall man, or a strong one for that. He was quite scrawny. He wouldn't have been able overpower a large man, but a woman…" Maybelle trailed off.

"The high heels…" Peter nodded.

Maybelle walked closer to the dented boxes and smiled over her shoulder at Peter. "And this, might just prove that our assailant was female."

Peter frowned as he looked to where Maybelle pointed. "Is that lipstick?"

Maybelle shrugged. "I can't be a hundred percent, but that sure looks like lipstick to me."

"We've been looking at men this the whole time. It seems we need to turn our focus to the fairer sex."

Maybelle nodded in agreement. "Definitely. Now the question is, why would the mayor have been alone in the storage room on a Friday night with a woman? Was he running around on the missus?"

Peter cringed. "I hope not. That's the worst news to deliver to a mourning family, that the victim was having an affair…"

"We don't know if it was an affair, but right now, it sure looks like it. This would be the perfect place to meet up. It's discreet, that's for sure."

"And it gives me the heebie jeebies—hardly romantic don't you think?"

Maybelle shrugged. "I've never had an affair, but I would think that discreet would trump romantic if you were town mayor."

"Let's think on this for a while and keep it to yourself, yeah?" Peter said as they left the storage room. He pulled off the crime scene tape and made the phone call the whole town had been waiting on.

The decorators could start preparing for the festival first thing in the morning.

[15]

CHRISTMAS COUNTDOWN – 10 DAYS UNTIL CHRISTMAS

Two black Cadillacs pulled into the cemetery at the edge of town, the black hearse driving in their wake.

Maybelle and Helen stood to one side as friends, family, and close business acquaintances surrounded the empty grave.

After an announcement in the Raven's Point gazette, it seemed that the entire town had come to a halt this morning to pay their last respects to the mayor. Most shop owners, like Maybelle and Helen, had closed their stores for the day out of respect and to attend the funeral.

The mourners parted as the mayor's wife and family approached the grave for the outdoor service they had chosen.

As they took their places at the side of the grave, six men lowered Andrew Hoffman's coffin onto bands that were spun across the grave, to lower the coffin after the service.

It was cold outside as frosty air from the north brought a fierce chill into town. Fierce enough that the town had to borrow a backhoe from a farmer with a frost bucket to dig the mayor's grave.

The dirt had been frozen solid.

Once the coffin was positioned, the pastor stepped to the head of the grave and opened his Bible. "Let us pray."

As the service began, Maybelle scanned who was in attendance. She recognized almost everyone and easily identified out-of-town mourners as well. The choice for the coffin flowers were probably made by the mayor's wife, and although calla lilies weren't Maybelle's favorite, they seemed sophisticated and masculine atop the cherry oak coffin.

It irked her that Andrew Hoffman was being buried today, and she and Peter had yet to find out who was responsible for his death. She wished they had more answers, but they weren't any closer to finding the mayor's killer than the day they had discovered his body.

This morning, on her way to the funeral she had driven past the town square. Usually when the decorations came up for the Christmas Festival, Maybelle would feel excited, but today she didn't feel that at all. Instead, it felt wrong for the town to just continue with its plans as if nothing had happened.

She met Peter's gaze where he stood on the opposite side of the grave and knew that he felt the same way she did.

They needed to solve this case, and soon.

The service wasn't long, thankfully, and the pastor had chosen thoughtful words to bid their mayor farewell. His wife delivered a short eulogy and explained that her husband had once told her that he preferred a graveside service than two sessions of mourning due to a loss.

Maybelle couldn't argue with his reasoning; she just wished it hadn't been winter.

Once the service had come to an end, Cecilia Hoffman stepped forward and sprinkled a hand of dried flower petals onto her husband's grave.

One by one, the mourners stepped forward and did the same as the coffin slowly began its descent into the ground.

"Ashes to ashes, dust to dust," someone said as they dropped their petals into the grave.

Somewhere behind her music played, a beautiful song about being in the arms of an angel. Although Maybelle hadn't been close to the mayor, the song brought tears to her eyes.

By the time she and Helen stepped up to the grave, Fiona, the town treasurer stood across from them. She wept heavily as she tossed some petals onto the coffin. When she looked up, the wind scooped her heavy bangs off her forehead revealing a nasty blue bruise.

Fiona quickly fixed her bangs before she smiled at Maybelle and walked away.

The after-service refreshments were being served at the Town Hall, and although Maybelle hadn't planned on going, Helen insisted that funeral sandwiches were the best.

"I can't believe you're into funeral sandwiches. Honestly, it's just depressing."

"It's not," Helen argued as they drove to Town Hall. "I don't know if it's the tears of the mourners making them, or because you're famished after being on your feet for so long, but it's definitely right up there with freshly baked donuts."

Maybelle chuckled. "And people think I'm odd."

"You are odd," Helen confirmed as she pulled up in front of Vintage on the Vine. "We can walk from here. I doubt there'll be any parking closer.

As they walked down Main Street, through the town square to the Town Hall, they were met with an assortment of decorations that had already been put up.

Peter was waiting for them at the entrance. "I was hoping you'd come. I don't have the guts to go at it alone."

"Are you here for the sandwiches?" Helen asked with a hint of a smile.

Peter nodded. "They're the best."

"See." Helen turned to Maybelle. "I told you. It isn't just me."

Maybelle rolled her eyes. "You're both a little cuckoo..." Maybelle caught sight of Fiona Charles and smiled at Helen. "Why don't you and Peter go on ahead, I quickly need to check something on my phone."

Once Peter and Helen were inside the Town Hall, Maybelle began to walk straight toward Fiona, with her eyes on her phone. She bumped into Fiona on purpose. When she looked up to apologize, her plan had worked perfectly. Fiona's bangs were disheveled revealing her scar.

"Oh, my goodness, I'm so sorry. I wasn't looking where I was going," Maybelle began to apologize. "You have a— Goodness... that's quite a bruise..."

Fiona quickly fixed her bangs. "It's nothing, really. Don't worry about bumping into me. We're all a little distracted today."

Fiona kept walking, but Maybelle quickly caught up. "How did you get it? It looks painful."

"It isn't painful at all. I think age is catching up with me, and that's why the bruise is so bad. I opened a kitchen cabinet without looking what I was doing and knocked it right into my head."

Maybelle smiled, although she didn't believe for a second that you could open a kitchen cabinet with such force. She fell back and resumed pretending to check on her phone when she heard someone else ask Fiona about her bruise.

"I'm so clumsy these days. I fell as I climbed out of the tub and knocked it on the sink." Fiona said shaking her head with a self-deprecating smile.

Maybelle's eyes narrowed. Regardless of how her sister insisted funeral sandwiches were the best, Maybelle wasn't heading into Town Hall for the sandwiches at all.

She didn't know why, but her gut instinct told her that she might just learn more than she had expected at the mayor's funeral.

Like who might be a likely suspect, one they hadn't even considered before.

One who had been there when the body was discovered.

And one who wore a very specific shade of red lipstick.

She wouldn't share her thoughts with Peter just yet. Instead, she helped herself to a cup of coffee and moved about the room, always remaining within earshot of Fiona Charles.

By the time Helen came to tell her that she was ready to leave, Fiona Charles had given two other explanations for her bruise and Maybelle still didn't believe one of them to be the truth.

Fiona was hiding something, that much Maybelle knew.

She just wasn't sure if it was a scuffle with the mayor or an abusive husband. But she knew as she followed Helen out of Town Hall, that she would start digging into Fiona the moment she got home.

You didn't get a bruise like that in a small town without everyone gossiping about what happened. And if you hid it, you usually had a very good reason.

[16]

CHRISTMAS COUNTDOWN – 8 DAYS UNTIL CHRISTMAS

Peter sat at his desk tapping his fingers to the beat of *Jaws*, wondering how much longer it was going to take before he received the extensive financial report on Fiona Charles.

After the funeral, Maybelle had pulled him to one side and told him about the bruise on her forehead and the shade of her lipstick. Both were probably just circumstantial, but right now, Peter had nothing more to go on to solve the mayor's murder than circumstantial evidence at best.

Although he couldn't make an arrest on anything circumstantial, it might lead him to more information or evidence that would lead him to the killer.

He couldn't believe that the town treasurer, respected by the entire town, was capable of murder. In his years of being a detective, he had seen the unlikeliest killers and knew that judging a book by its cover or social reputation was in most cases misleading.

Peter hit the refresh button on his emails again and let out a sigh as the little circle went round and round as it retrieved any new emails.

The email from the forensic financial unit hit his inbox like a glowing red flag, making him smile. He clicked it open, hit the print button and rubbed his hands together as anticipation washed over him. He didn't know why, but the fact that the report took more than a day to reach him made him hopeful that there was something there that Fiona Charles wouldn't want anyone to know.

Peter read the quick report the accountant attached and set it aside before he went through the statements himself. The more he read, the more he realized he might just have caught a larger fish than he imagined.

If Fiona Charles had something to do with Andrew Hoffman's murder, he was bound to find something here. He turned over the page and discovered even more irregularities. He began to note dates and expenses before going back even more and discovering exactly what he had suspected.

Less than a year ago, Fiona Charles had been flat broke, with outstanding credit bills that would've forced her to sell her house.

Then suddenly, a month later, a large amount was deposited into her account and the debts were settled. For a couple of months, the expenses were nothing out of the ordinary until another large amount was deposited.

This time the money was used to buy a new car, what seemed to be a shopping spree of online retailers, followed by salon and spa treatments.

After that, a large sum was deposited every month but almost as soon as it cleared, it was transferred out again. The transfers out of the account were a little hard to follow, so Peter returned to the report from the forensic accountant.

He saw another email had entered his inbox, and he opened it up.

A sly smile curved his mouth as he shook his head. "Small towns have hound dogs too…"

It turned out that Fiona Charles had realized that spending her money from a US bank account could land her in hot water, so instead she had gone ahead and opened an offshore account.

The balance in the offshore account made Peter gasp.

Apparently, it paid to be a civil servant in a small town, unless Fiona Charles had begun selling something illegal on the side.

A phone call distracted him from the statements in front of him. He had suspected it, but the phone call confirmed that Nicolas Evans had an alibi for the night of the mayor's murder. This time, Peter didn't mind losing a suspect at all, because he had a feeling his new suspect was much more fitting to the crime.

The only question was, where did Fiona Charles's sudden tidal wave of money come from?

[17]

WHILE PETER WAS INVESTIGATING Fiona's financials, Maybelle decided to do a little investigation of her own.

After the funeral, she was convinced that Fiona's bruise had nothing to do with a fall, a cupboard door, or even a stray ball from the park. She didn't know why, but she had a feeling that there was more to Fiona Charles than just her a new car and her new bruise.

If there was one way you wanted to find out what was going on in a small town, you talked to the secretaries. Secretaries were the people who were hired to keep secrets and to know everything about their boss's business, although not everyone made sure their secretaries knew how to hold their tongue.

As Maybelle walked into the municipal offices at the Town Hall, she hoped that would be the case when it came to Andrew Hoffman's secretary.

She had a stack of paperwork under her arm as an excuse as she walked right to the mayor's office.

"Hello, can I help you?" the secretary, a young blonde, asked with a cheerful smile.

Maybelle shrugged and let out a helpless sigh. "Yes, please. I think I'm lost. I need to file some property taxes, and I seem to get lost in this maze of offices every time."

"No problem, you just go straight down the hall, then there's a washroom, first door to your right after the washroom, although I think Macey's on lunch at the moment," the blonde said with a frown.

Maybelle nodded. "Thanks… I can't imagine how awkward it must be for you to still man his desk when he's not…here."

"It's hard, but someone needs to do it. We can't just let the phone ring—what if the governor calls?"

"Yes, of course. I can't stop thinking about it though. I mean everyone liked him. I couldn't imagine Mayor Hoffman even getting angry. But then I didn't work with him as closely as you did," Maybelle finished unapologetically.

The secretary nodded. "He was a very docile man, but there has been a time or two when I could hear the anger in his voice."

"Really?" Maybelle leaned closer. "When was that? Or should I rather ask who was he furious at?"

The secretary glanced over Maybelle's shoulder to make sure no one was in the hall before she spoke. "The first time it was with the contractor that had to repaint Town Hall. Mayor Hoffman insisted on having it painted a dove grey and when the contractor began painting, after having purchased gallons and gallons of paint, it was charcoal."

Maybelle flinched. "That would've looked like an eyesore on Main Street."

"Exactly. Mayor Hoffman made it very clear that the paint would be replaced with the right color at the expense of the contractor, or he would make sure that his contracting license was pulle,d and he never worked in Raven's Point again."

"Harsh, but fair." Maybelle smiled approvingly. "And the other time?"

"Oh, that was just... the Friday he... that Friday." The secretary shook her head. "Miss Charles, the treasurer, was in his office. He had been trying to make an appointment for her for weeks before he finally managed to pin down a time that suited them both. They were barely in there for ten minutes before they began to argue. I couldn't hear what it was about, but Mayor Hoffman was very angry. Miss Charles stormed out, slamming the door after her. For the next hour the mayor was huffing and puffing in his office, muttering to himself about trust."

Maybelle almost smiled—this proved exactly what she thought it would. Fiona Charles was involved in some way; she wasn't sure how or what the motive was, but she now knew for sure that they parted on bad terms on Friday afternoon, and by Friday night at ten o'clock the mayor had been murdered.

Knowing exactly what she needed to do next, Maybelle left Town Hall and headed straight to the station. She had a feeling this information would be crucial to whatever Peter had found on Fiona.

[18]

"And you're sure about this?" Peter asked as he paced his office.

"Yes. The mayor's secretary said that he muttered about trust for the rest of the afternoon. And that Fiona Charles was livid when she left his office."

With what he had discovered with Fiona's financial reports, Peter suddenly realized where the money might have come from. He didn't voice his suspicions to Maybelle just yet, wanting to confirm it first.

"She doesn't have a weapon," Peter muttered to himself.

Maybelle shrugged. "Really, that's what you're going on?"

"No, it isn't, I'm just pointing out the obvious. Wait, how did you get the secretary to be so forthcoming with what she told you?" Peter asked curiously.

Maybelle smiled, making his heart skip a beat. "I pretended to be lost on my way to file property taxes. I offered her my condolences and the conversation just happened to take on a direction of its own."

"Maybelle Wright, you're a master manipulator when it comes to making a conversation take a direction of *your* choosing." Peter shook his head with a teasing smile.

"Now we have the lipstick, the bruise on the head, and we have a witness who saw them having an argument."

"We still don't know how she got the bruise." Peter hated playing devil's advocate, but he had to. "How do we confirm that she obtained that bruise on the night the mayor was killed?"

Maybelle shrugged. "I have no idea, but I just know that it was her. But what I don't know is why she did it."

Peter shrugged. "I think I have a hunch, but I want to make sure of it first. Tell me this, has she ever been married?"

"Not that I know of. I think she was engaged once, but it didn't stick. For as long as I can remember, Fiona Charles has been single."

"That means no alimony...." Peter muttered to himself.

Maybelle frowned. "Alimony?"

"Never mind. I have a few things to take care of. I'll stop by as soon as I know something."

"Yeah, I better get back to the store. The Christmas Festival is starting tomorrow, and Helen and I need to get everything ready before we set up tomorrow morning."

"Good luck, and tell Helen I said hi."

Maybelle nodded with a smile before she walked out of his office. Peter waited for a whole ten minutes before he grabbed his coat, asked the chief to join him, and headed to Town Hall.

If what he thought had been the case was the case, there was only one way to prove it, and he had a feeling it wouldn't be very hard to prove once he got his hands on the right paperwork.

"Are you sure I need to go with?" the chief complained as he walked with Peter.

Peter nodded. "I don't have a warrant, but I do have the key. I need you there to back me up if anyone tries to stop me."

"They won't stop you, not if I'm there." The Chief puffed out his chest with pride.

"Exactly."

Peter walked through the doors of the administration offices that were adjacent to Town Hall. He glanced at the chief and headed straight for the mayor's office. Hopefully, the secretary would be just as forthcoming with him as she had been with Fiona.

[19]

CHRISTMAS COUNTDOWN – 7 DAYS TO CHRISTMAS

The morning of the festival, Maybelle and Helen were up at five am.

After collecting everything for their stall from Vintage on the Vine, they headed to the town square and began to set up. By eight o'clock, their stall was transformed into a magical rendition of everything Christmas, both old and new.

The two life-sized nutcrackers stood at the entrance of their stall, with more of their little friends distributed throughout.

When the festival officially opened at nine o'clock, with a welcome speech delivered by Fiona Charles in the absence of a mayor, Maybelle and Helen were running high on caffeine and excitement for the day.

The team of decorators had done an exceptional job of decorating the square and the park for the festival. This year's theme was Winter Wonderland, with everything silver and magical. Fairy lights were strung on every surface, even over the square to create a mystical roof of stars.

It was better than any festival before.

Although Maybelle was excited for the festival, she was still irked about Fiona Charles. She had a gut feeling that Fiona was involved, but she didn't know how to prove it. She couldn't help but hope that Peter managed to find out more after she stopped by to see him.

"Maybelle, if you keep frowning at all the customers, no one is going to come into our stall." Helen poked Maybelle's shoulder with a narrowed look.

"I'm not frowning, I'm thinking," Maybelle insisted.

Helen cocked a brow. "You've been frowning all morning. Although you're here and you did your part, you're not in the spirit of Christmas at all. Heck, I even had to remind you to feed the chickens before we left. You've never forgotten to feed the chickens," Helen reminded her.

Maybelle shrugged. "I'm sorry, Helen. It's just this thing with the mayor, it's really bothering me. I can't help but feel as Peter and I failed him somehow. The Christmas Festival has officially started, and the murderer is still walking free."

"I've known you too long, and you've been involved in too many investigations to hide anything from me. I know you know who did it, and the reason why you're in a bad mood is because you can't prove it. So, who is it?" Helen demanded in a whisper.

Maybelle took a few steps backing up deeper into the stall. She turned to Helen with a narrowed look. "Fiona Charles."

Helen gasped. "What?"

"Helen, quiet!" Maybelle quickly hushed her sister.

"Sorry, I just can't imagine… She's the image of the perfect lady. Giving her time to the community by being a civil servant, always the icon of style…" Helen trailed off shaking her head.

Maybelle rolled her eyes. "You do realize that criminals don't wear a scarlet 'C' on their shirts or blouses?"

Helen sighed. "You can put the sarcasm away, thank you."

"I'm sorry. It's just… I know it's her. I can feel it in my veins, and here she is this morning taking the podium when it should've been Mayor Hoffman."

"I take it you and Peter have nothing to tie her to the murder just yet?" Helen asked curiously before her face transformed into a bright smile. "Season greetings! Welcome to the home of nutcrackers, ballerinas, vintage decorations and all things Christmas."

Maybelle quickly turned around with a smile in place. "All the nutcrackers are sold in pairs, and we also have some vintage glass baubles if you'd be interested."

"And vintage tree toppers. Nothing like a tree topper to pass down as a family heirloom," Helen added.

Their conversation was halted as their first customer was followed by the second and the third, until Maybelle stopped keeping count.

Before she knew it, two hours had flown by, and they had sold half a dozen of the nutcrackers. Apparently, the nutcracker theme had been a wonderful idea.

Maybelle kept checking her phone to see if Peter had tried to reach her, but there were no new messages or missed calls. She wasn't sure if it was because he was still digging, or because he simply couldn't find anything to tie Fiona to the murder.

"Maybelle, customer for you." Helen nodded towards the entrance of the stall, before she turned back to help the customer she had been helping.

Maybelle turned with her perfect saleslady smile in place, only to be faced with Peter. Her heart skipped a beat, the rush of attraction almost making her forget why she wanted to see him.

"Hello," Maybelle finally found her voice.

"Merry Christmas, or should I ask what's with the nutcracker?" Peter asked with a teasing grin.

Maybelle laughed. "It's our theme. Awesome, isn't it?"

Peter nodded. "It's original. I'll give you that. Can we talk for a minute?"

Maybelle nodded. "Sure."

She led him away from Helen and her customer to the back of the stall where they kept their extra stock. "What did you find?"

Peter's mouth curved into a smile. "Everything she hoped I wouldn't. I've got a warrant for the DNA sample to match with the lipstick we found in the storage room. I thought we could do this quietly, but the mayor deserved better."

"What do you have in mind?" Maybelle asked with a mischievous smile.

Peter told her what he found before he told Maybelle that the mayor deserved this traitor to be publicly humiliated, and if he was lucky, she'd even give him a public confession.

Maybelle couldn't stop the adrenalin from rushing through her veins. "You want to do it now?"

Peter nodded. "Can Helen spare you?"

"She can," Maybelle promised. After a quick word with Helen, Maybelle and Peter set off in search of Fiona Charles. She wasn't sure who was more determined to make Fiona shrivel with humiliation, she or Peter.

But after killing their mayor in cold blood only because he learned the truth, she deserved nothing less.

[20]

Maybelle followed Peter as they weaved their way through the stalls, the coffee vendors and food trucks, to the center of the square where Fiona was probably playing the role of mayor and welcoming visitors at the entrance to the market.

Just as suspected, she had taken it upon herself to act in the absence of a mayor and was welcoming everyone with a bright smile, donning that familiar shade of lipstick that would be the evidence they needed to tie her to the murder.

"She thinks she got away with it," Maybelle muttered under her breath.

"Yup, she thinks we're as clueless as she is about us being onto her," Peter agreed.

"How do you want to do this?" Maybelle asked.

"Just follow my lead," Peter said over his shoulder as he walked right up to Fiona Charles.

"Detective, how nice of you to come and support our little soiree," Fiona said with a beaming smile for Peter, ignoring Maybelle completely.

"Hello, Fiona," Maybelle stepped forward with a frosty smile.

"Maybelle, isn't it? I saw your stall earlier. I'm sure you're going to reap in record sales this year." Fiona returned her gaze to Peter. "I was hoping to speak to you. Have you made any progress on the investigation?"

Peter cleared his throat before he spoke, a little louder than necessary. "Actually, we've made quite an inroad with the investigation on the mayor's murder."

"Really, have you?" Fiona asked, batting her lashes—the only sign that she was slightly nervous.

"Yes. As it turns out," Peter rose his voice a little more and Maybelle could see the curious townsfolk start to turn and pay attention. "The mayor confronted someone the evening of his murder. Feeling trapped, the person he confronted decided that it would be better for them if the mayor couldn't repeat his accusations, or rather his accurate findings, to anyone else."

"Oh, my goodness, that's just terrible. Do you have any idea who this person might have been?" Fiona asked with wide eyes.

Peter nodded. "Yes. We do."

For a moment you could cut the air between Fiona and Peter with a blunt knife as tension filled the space.

"Cut it out, Fiona, we know it was you," Maybelle finally couldn't stop herself from spilling the beans.

Fiona began to laugh hysterically. "Me? You think I killed the mayor?"

Peter nodded. Maybelle could see that he was chuffed that his loud voice had gathered quite the crowd.

"Yes. You see, it's strange what you find when you start digging into someone's life, especially their financial records. Isn't it just amazing how after finding yourself on the edge of bankruptcy, you suddenly managed to pay all your debts, buy a new car, and go on a number of shopping sprees, both online and local?"

"You're reaching," Fiona muttered through her teeth.

"Am I?" Peter shook his head. "I doubt it, because as it happens, every large sum of money deposited into your account, happened to be paid from the town's coffers. And when you realized how easy it was to steal from the good folks of Raven's Point, you couldn't stop yourself, could you? You opened an account in the Caymans and promptly started sending all the money you stole there. You thought money in the Caymans would be untraceable and untouchable by the government, right?"

Fiona's eyes widened with horror. "You can't prove it was me..."

"Oh, but I can. You see it might take a while and a few legal hoops to retrieve the money you tried to hide in the Caymans, but in the end, the town will get it back, every penny."

"You still can't prove I killed the mayor. Committing fraud and killing someone are two different things."

"Yes, they are. But you see, after having investigated quite a few cases in my time, I've often learned to look past the obvious. Like your bruise for example... Remind me again what happened?"

"I fell getting out of the tub at home," Fiona quickly answered.

"Really, you told me you bumped it on a kitchen cabinet." Maybelle cocked a brow.

"She told me she walked into a sign on Main Street," someone piped up from the crowd.

"See, you need to keep your lies straight for them to work. Then, of course," Peter smiled as he gestured at her mouth before pointing to her feet, "there is the evidence of your lipstick found in the storage room, with your high heeled shoe print."

"You can't prove it was me," Fiona argued, taking a step back.

"Correct me if I'm wrong, but here's what I believe happened. The mayor caught on that you were helping yourself to the town coffers. He tried to make a meeting with you, but you kept turning him down, claiming to be too busy. That Friday afternoon, you argued in his office, because he confronted you about it. You rushed out angrily. I'm right so far?" Peter asked before he continued, not giving her chance to answer.

"On your way home later that evening you noticed the mayor's car in front of town square. You knew he'd be checking to make sure everything was ready to set up for the Christmas Festival the following morning. It was the perfect opportunity for you to talk to him in private, to beg him not to give you over to the police. At least, that was what you hoped."

Maybelle stepped forward.

"May I?" she asked Peter, who nodded before she turned to Maybelle. "So, you went in, begged him to forgive you, probably even promised to pay back every penny, if he'd just keep it quiet. But Mayor Hoffman wasn't being as flexible as you thought he'd be; in fact, my guess is he was furious. He told you that he would be turning you in, probably Monday morning first thing. The idea of going to jail, the humiliation... it was just too much for you. So, you pulled out the 9mm revolver you inherited from your father and never bothered to license to your name. You shot him, in the shoulder, but he didn't go down. Instead, he came after you..."

Fiona's face went pale, her mouth opening and closing like a fish gasping for air.

"He tried to get the gun away from you, but in the scuffle, you fell over some boxes. You bumped your head against the wall, and left behind some of... what shade is that exactly..."

"It's Harleton Red," someone called out from the crowd. "She buys it from me at the drugstore."

"Thanks." Peter smiled at the woman in the crowd before he turned back to Fiona. "And it's that Harleton Red, that's going to prove you were there. You managed to get back on your feet and run, but you stopped, just long enough to shoot him again, this time in the heart."

"You panicked." Maybelle sighed. "So, you locked the door, took the mayor's keys and pretended like nothing happened at all. You probably still have the keys, don't you, Fiona?"

Fiona's face flushed crimson red.

"Check her purse!" a man called out from the growing crowd.

"Fine! I did it! I didn't mean to. It was self-defense, I was afraid he was going to hurt me." Fiona began to cry.

"No, you weren't afraid he was going to hurt you, you were afraid he was going to ruin your reputation." Peter nodded. "Fiona Charles, I have a warrant for a sample of your DNA, and you are under arrest for the murder of Mayor Andrew Hoffman."

The crowd applauded as Peter took Fiona by the arm and led her to the waiting patrol vehicle he had on standby.

[21]

CHRISTMAS DAY

"Do you think we know what we're doing?" Helen asked, glancing around the dining room.

Maybelle nodded without hesitation. "Of course, we know what we're doing. We're doing Christmas lunch, our way, with our friends."

"I know that, but aren't there like, some things they'd expect? I know Grandma always made bread pudding," Helen said, fussing with the napkins.

"Helen, honoring the traditions Grandma gave us is one thing, but that doesn't mean we have to try and recreate what she did. If she were here now, I guarantee you she'd love how we're doing Christmas lunch... with a twist."

Helen shrugged. "Ugly sweaters and all?"

"Ugly sweaters and all." Maybelle agreed before giving her sister a hug. "Merry Christmas, Helen."

Their grandmother, Mabel Francine Wright, who had left them the old Victorian home, had collected ugly Christmas sweaters as a hobby. She had even knitted a few over the years. In honor of her, both Maybelle and Helen were wearing Christmas sweaters, and they had even laid out sweaters for their guests as well.

The doorbell began to chime jingle bells, and Helen's face lit up. "They're here."

Maybelle added a few more pieces of popcorn to the two-foot-long platter she had prepared. There was a variety of chopped carrots, kale, broccoli and even raw pumpkin along with an assortment of seeds.

"Please tell me that's not our lunch," Peter said, joining her in the kitchen with a bottle of wine in his hand.

Maybelle laughed. "We did cook, if that's what you mean. This is for Albert and the gang."

"You made a Christmas lunch platter for your chickens?" Peter asked, baffled.

Helen laughed as she and her friend, Ava, the medical examiner joined them in the kitchen. "You try and stop her. I couldn't."

"Just because they don't understand Christmas, doesn't mean they don't get to share in the festivities." Maybelle shrugged defensively.

"Is that turkey I smell?" Ava asked with an excited smile.

"Yup, I made it." Helen smiled proudly. "Grandma Mabel's recipe."

"It smells delicious," Peter agreed.

"Come on, you have to put on your ugly sweater." Helen all but dragged Ava out of the kitchen to the dining room.

"Ugly sweater?" Peter asked with a frown.

Maybelle nodded. "Helen and I are creating a few traditions of our own."

"Like the life-size nutcracker dolls standing beside the fireplace?" Peter chuckled shaking his head.

"We got them for the market, but I simply couldn't sell them. They look awesome, don't they?" Maybelle asked with a smile. "You brought wine?"

"Yes, a twenty-five-year-old burgundy. Since you said no gifts, I thought I'd contribute another way."

"Contribution appreciated." Maybelle beamed as she opened the drawer to take out the corkscrew. When she turned around Peter was standing only a couple of feet from her.

Her heart skipped a beat with anticipation. Both she and Peter had agreed to only be friends, but when he was so close that she could smell his cologne and feel his body heat, the word friendship didn't come to mind.

"I think that some traditions should be honored, don't you?" Peter asked glancing up.

Maybelle couldn't stop the smile that curved her mouth. Above their heads, in the space between them, Peter held a piece of mistletoe. She met his gaze and felt that familiar attraction she had tried to fight against so many times in the past.

"Peter?" Maybelle asked hesitantly.

Peter shrugged. "It is a tradition."

Maybelle laughed softly as she leaned in. She expected it to be a brief brush of lips, but instead, it was as if the earth and the sun collided, and a thousand stars were born the moment their lips touched. Her heart skipped a beat, making her want to linger a little longer, but she finally managed to pull away.

Peter met her surprised look with a satisfied smile. "Didn't expect that, did you?"

Maybelle laughed. "I've come to expect the unexpected from you."

"I've come to expect the same from you. Wine first, or should we serve the chickens their Christmas lunch?"

The fact that he asked, made Maybelle like him even more. "I think the chickens can start celebrating Christmas, that way no one will try and fly the coop and steal the wine."

Their laughter blended in the air as they walked to the dining room where Ava and Helen were waiting. As Peter served the wine, Maybelle took a moment to take it all in.

It wasn't a Christmas like the ones they usually had with their grandmother, but it was unique in every single way. And she found that she quite liked it.

The End

CONTINUE READING...

Thank you for reading **Death by Christmas Festival! Are you wondering what to read next?** Why not read *Holiday Death by Drowning*? **Here's a sneak peek for you:**

"Do we have more tinsel in the back?" Helen Wright asked, precariously balancing her weight on a crate as she attached a string of tinsel to a tall shelf.

Maybelle was about to answer her sister, but a sudden text brought a smile to her face and sent Helen's request miles from her mind.

I've had a bad day, seeing your face will light up the day like a Christmas tree. Meet me over lunch at the diner?

Maybelle's heart fluttered slightly at his charming, yet cheesy, words. But if Christmas wasn't the season for silly and cheesy, when was? Besides, she couldn't remember the last time a handsome, successful, attractive man had made her feel this way—as giddy as a teenager on the night of the prom.

She tilted her head as she began texting him back. But before she could hit send or even finish typing the message, Helen's shrill voice sliced through the Christmas carols that played from their grandmother's turntable in the corner.

"Maybelle Wright! I swear if I fall and break my neck because you're going gaga over a text, I will make you wash, dress, and feed me for eternity!"

Maybelle looked up and noticed her sister's dangerous position. "Helen! Get down from there. You'll break your neck!"

"If I had some help, I wouldn't have to endanger my life to bring a little Christmas spirit to the shop. But apparently you have more important things on your mind, or should I say a certain sexy developer?" Helen sniped back.

"I'm sorry, you know how it is after the first date." Maybelle got to her feet, apology in her eyes, although her smile was still giddy. "The texts, the innuendos, the flirting..."

"I would love to know how it is after the first date, Maybelle, but I haven't dated anyone in more than a year. Could you put Drake on hold and fetch me the tinsel, please?" Helen climbed down from the crate, grabbing onto a shelf for dear life as her knees still quivered from balancing her stance.

Click Here to Continue Reading!
https://ticahousepublishing.com/cozy-mystery.html

THANKS FOR READING

If you love Cozy Mysteries, **Click Here**

https://cozymystery.subscribemenow.com/

to hear about all **New Donna Muse Mystery Releases! I will let you know as soon as they become available!**

Thank you, Friends! If you enjoyed **Death by Christmas Festival,** would you kindly take a couple minutes to leave a positive review on Amazon? It only takes a moment, and positive reviews truly make a difference. Thank you so much! I appreciate it!

Much love,

Donna Muse

MORE DONNA MUSE COZY MYSTERIES!

We love quirky Cozy Mysteries and are building a library of Donna Muse titles just for you!
(Remember that ALL of Donna's titles can be downloaded FREE with Kindle Unlimited!)

CLICK HERE to discover Donna's Complete Collection of Cozy Mysteries!
https://ticahousepublishing.com/cozy-mystery.html

ABOUT THE AUTHOR

Donna Muse has been a mystery buff for years! But she hasn't been a fan of blood and gore. So when the Cozy Mystery genre came into being, she jumped on board with both feet. She loves the amateur sleuth and is fascinated by the intense and often comical way the perpetrator is revealed. Donna lives in Maine with her husband, loves walking by the surf, fishing for striped bass, and playing with her grandchildren and her cats.

contact@ticahousepublishing.com

Printed in Dunstable, United Kingdom